or more of the following negligent acts in the treatment of breaking the cookie in alleged equal parts:

a. Did negligently and carelessly and unskillfully fail to possess and to exercise the proper, adequate, and customary knowledge and skill required of fair cookie splitting;

b. Did negligently and carelessly and unskillfully fail to possess and to exercise the proper, adequate, and customary knowledge and skill required of the simple concept of sharing;

c. Did deliberately amplify the injurious effect of his actions by seeking to dismiss said negligence with the defense: "That's the way the cookie crumbles."

d. Which, by the way, was very annoying and not one bit funny;

7. That as a direct and proximate result of one or more of the foregoing acts or omissions of negligence, the Plaintiff, Sibling No. 1, suffered grievous emotional trauma and malnourishment.

WHEREFORE, Plaintiff, Half No. 1, by and through Fullglass and Milk, P.C., states for the record "no fair" and prays for judgment against the Defendant, Half No. 2.

Respectfully submitted,
Fullglass and Milk, P.C.

Jason B. Rosenthal, Esq.

cc: Mom[1]

---

[1] You are so busted when she finds out.

It's Not

AMY KROUSE ROSENTHAL

TOM LICHTENHELD

HarperCollins*Publishers*

Why'd I get the smaller half?

Why'd he get the bigger laugh?

Why can't I have a pet giraffe?

Why can't I have curly locks?

Why can't I have my own box?

Why now, chicken pox?

It's not fair.

You get to
stay up late?
I've got to go
up at eight.

They said they would but didn't wait.

It's not fair.

Why don't
you yell
at her?

Hey, it was my turn to stir!

I don't know; it's all a blur.

It's not fair.

Why does she get brand-new shoes?

Why does my team always lose?

Why'd he get
an extra leg?

Why am I the sole
square peg?

Why am I always
bottom bunk?

How come she gets all the rings?

Why do birds get all the wings?

Why can't books
go on and on?
No more endings,
only Once Upons . . .

The End.

Why's Mom only dedicating this to Miles?

It's not fair. . . .

—A.K.R.

To Jan, for her patience, inspiration, and love

—T.L.

Special thank-you to Paris Rosenthal for putting in the last word.

kook productions

amy krouse rosenthal & tom lichtenheld

It's Not Fair!

Text copyright © 2008 by Amy Krouse Rosenthal

Illustrations copyright © 2008 by Tom Lichtenheld

Manufactured in China.

www.harpercollinschildrens.com

Library of Congress Cataloging-in-Publication Data is available.

ISBN 978-0-06-115257-3 (trade bdg.) — ISBN 978-0-06-115258-0 (lib. bdg.)

Typography by Jeanne L. Hogle

1 2 3 4 5 6 7 8 9 10

❖

First Edition

IN THE CIRCUIT COURT OF FAIRNESS

LAW DEPARTMENT – LAW DIVISION

SIBLING NO. 1,)
)
)
)
Plaintiff)
)
)
—vs.—) Case No.: AKR 030291
)
SIBLING NO. 2,)
)
)
Defendant)
)

COMPLAINT AT LAW

Now comes Sibling No. 1, by and through its attorneys, Fullglass and Milk, P.C., and for its totally unfair cause of action against Defendant, Sibling No. 2, states as follows:

1. That on or about, to wit: the day before yesterday, the Plaintiff, Sibling No. 1, clearly got the smaller half of the cookie.

2. That on or about, to wit: the day before yesterday, and at all other relevant times, the Defendant, Sibling No. 2, said that he would break the cookie right down the middle.

3. That on or about, to wit: the day before yesterday, and at all other relevant times, the Plaintiff, Sibling No. 1, relied—to his dismay and detriment—on the assertion that the Defendant, Sibling No. 2, would indeed break the cookie perfectly in half.

4. That on or about, to wit: the day before yesterday and at all other relevant times, and in reliance thereon, there was in full force and effect an expectation that the cookie would be split in equal shares, with the chocolate chips being distributed equally between the two halves.

5. That on or about, to wit: the day before yesterday, and at all other relevant times, the Plaintiff, Sibling No. 1, in fact received the way smaller half.

6. That despite the aforementioned duty, the Defendant, Sibling No. 2, was then and there guilty of one